SO-DTA-065

KIDS CAN'T STOP READING
THE CHOOSE YOUR
OWN ADVENTURE® STORIES!

"Choose Your Own Adventure is the best thing that has come along since books themselves."
—Alysha Beyer, age 11

"I didn't read much before, but now I read my Choose Your Own Adventure books almost every night."
—Chris Brogan, age 13

"I love the control I have over what happens next."
—Kosta Efstathiou, age 17

"Choose Your Own Adventure books are so much fun to read and collect—I want them all!"
—Brendan Davin, age 11

And teachers like this series, too:

"We have read and reread, worn thin, loved, loaned, bought for others, and donated to school libraries our Choose Your Own Adventure books."

CHOOSE YOUR OWN ADVENTURE®—
AND MAKE READING MORE FUN!

STAMPEDE!

BY LABAN CARRICK HILL

ILLUSTRATED BY ERIC CHERRY

An R. A. Montgomery Book

BANTAM BOOKS
NEW YORK • TORONTO • LONDON • SYDNEY • AUCKLAND

RL 4, ages 8–12

STAMPEDE!

A Bantam Book / November 1997

*CHOOSE YOUR OWN ADVENTURE® is a registered trademark
of Bantam Books, a division of Bantam Doubleday Dell
Publishing Group, Inc.
Registered in U.S. Patent and Trademark Office
and elsewhere.*

Original conception of Edward Packard

*Cover art by Romas Kukalis
Interior illustrations by Eric Cherry*

*All rights reserved.
Copyright © 1997 by R. A. Montgomery
Cover art and illustrations copyright © 1997 by
Bantam Books.
No part of this book may be reproduced or transmitted in any
form or by any means, electronic or mechanical, including photo-
copying, recording, or by any information storage and retrieval
system, without permission in writing from the publisher.
For information address: Bantam Books.*

*If you purchased this book without a cover you should be aware
that this book is stolen property. It was reported as "unsold and
destroyed" to the publisher and neither the author nor the publisher has received any payment for this "stripped book."*

ISBN 0-553-56756-X

Published simultaneously in the United States and Canada

*Bantam Books are published by Bantam Books, a division of
Bantam Doubleday Dell Publishing Group, Inc. Its trademark,
consisting of the words "Bantam Books" and the portrayal of a
rooster, is Registered in U.S. Patent and Trademark Office and in
other countries. Marca Registrada. Bantam Books, 1540
Broadway, New York, New York 10036.*

PRINTED IN THE UNITED STATES OF AMERICA
CWO   0 9 8 7 6 5 4 3 2 1

STAMPEDE!

WARNING!

This book is not like other books you have read. In this story, *you* choose what happens next. There are many different endings, so you can read this book over and over again, and it will be different every time.

As you read, you'll have the chance to decide what will happen. Whenever you make a decision, turn to the page shown. What happens to you next in the story depends on your choices.

One choice means you get to go on a cattle drive, which will be full of surprises. Another choice means you'll stay at the ranch to help break some wild mustangs. Make your choice carefully—the West is still wild!

It's your choice. Your thrills. *Your* adventure!

You're in a window seat on a plane to Salt Lake City, Utah. Summer vacation began yesterday, and you're going to spend it with your uncle Brad and aunt Lucy. You've been up in the air two hours, and you still have one hour to go.

Outside, white clouds, like massive balls of cotton, appear to carry the plane along. The ride has been pretty smooth, and you've kept busy looking out the window, reading magazines, and drinking the extra cartons of orange juice the flight attendant gave you. But now you're getting bored. You can't wait to land in Salt Lake City.

This is the first time you've visited Uncle Brad and Aunt Lucy at their place. And you're very excited because they own a cattle ranch, the Anchor P.

You pull Uncle Brad's letter out of your pocket and read it for the millionth time.

Hey, kiddo!
I've got to drive my beeves down off Hurricane Cliffs to Cedar City. I could use a steady cowhand rounding up strays. How about it? Come down when school lets out.

Love,
Uncle Brad

→

2

When you first read the letter you had to ask your dad what a "beeve" was. Your dad smiled and said a beef was a beef steer.

Now you pull out your map of Utah and look at the southwestern corner of the state, where Hurricane Cliffs runs north and south. That's where Uncle Brad's cattle have been grazing for the last few months. Hurricane Cliffs is a national park with public grazing land. Cedar City isn't more than a couple of inches away from the park on the map. It doesn't seem far, but your dad has assured you that it is indeed a long ride.

The sound of static over the plane's intercom interrupts your thoughts. The pilot's voice comes over the speaker, announcing, "Fasten your seat belts and adjust your seats in an upright position. We will be landing in approximately ten minutes."

You close your eyes and imagine what a beef looks like up close. Before you know it, the plane has landed and is taxiing up to the terminal. When it's time to get off the plane, you hurry through the exit and immediately spot Uncle Brad in the terminal.

Actually it's not hard to find Uncle Brad. He's head and shoulders above everyone else, and he's wearing the largest, most outrageous cowboy hat you've ever seen. It's a black ten-gallon hat with dozens of feathers sticking out of a bright red band.

→

"Howdy, pardner!" Uncle Brad yells at you through the crowd.

You wave to him and squeeze through the crush of people.

Uncle Brad slaps you on the back. "Well, now, you must be four inches bigger than when I saw you at Grammy's last Christmas. You're gonna need that extra size to handle old Rosie."

"Who's old Rosie?" you ask nervously.

"Why, old Rosie is the horse I have waiting for you. She's a nice friendly ride, but sometimes she gets stubborn and you have to show her who's boss."

You swallow. The only horses you've ridden have been at summer camp. And even though you were one of the best riders at camp, you never rode outside the corral. You get the feeling that riding a horse out on the range is a lot different.

"Let's grab your gear and head back to the Anchor P," Uncle Brad says. "It's a three-hour drive."

You follow him to the baggage claim carousels and grab your suitcase. You wanted to bring only a knapsack, but your mom insisted on packing just about everything you own. She kept saying, "You never know. It's better to be prepared."

→

4

As you lift the monster suitcase, you decide that you never want to be this prepared again in your life.

On the drive you fall asleep. You don't wake up until you hit the red shale road leading up to the ranch. "Are we there?" you ask, rubbing your eyes.

"Just about," Uncle Brad answers.

On both sides of the road, rolling foothills extend as far as you can see. There isn't a building or house in sight. The only sign of life is the ribbon of dirt road that lies ahead.

"Where are the cows?" you ask.

Uncle Brad laughs. "They're not cows. They're cattle. Cows are for milkin', cattle's for eatin'." He points out his side window to a massive wall of cliffs that crops out beyond a long stretch of hills. "Up there in those foothills there are about a thousand head of cattle."

"Wow!" you gasp. You didn't realize your aunt and uncle's ranch was so large.

"Don't be too impressed," Uncle Brad says. "There are plenty of ranches much larger than mine. In fact, there are some agribusinesses out here with around five to ten thousand head of cattle. So this is a small operation. And we need all the help we can get, which is why I'm so glad you came." He slaps you on the back again, nearly knocking the breath from you.

→

As you come over a hill, you see the Anchor P. It's made up of six buildings: a nice-looking white clapboard house with a porch, three barns, a bunkhouse, and an equipment shed.

"All this is yours?" you ask in surprise. You've never known anyone to own so many buildings and so much land. You live in a small apartment in the city with your parents and little sister.

"Yup," Uncle Brad answers. "This here is the main house, where Aunt Lucy and I live. And over here is the bunkhouse, where the crew beds."

Just then three scruffy-looking people come riding up to the bunkhouse, waving their hats over their heads.

Uncle Brad waves his arm out the window. "Hey, come over and meet our new cowhand."

Stepping from the cab of the truck, Uncle Brad introduces his crew. "This here is Walter. He's the best roper in Utah, and he's our trail boss."

A tall, lanky fellow with a handlebar mustache takes his hat off and nods when you say hello.

"This is Muddy." Your uncle points to a small but muscular-looking woman with long, dark hair pulled back in a ponytail. "She's not much good for anything but eating us out of house and home. We put up with her anyway."

→

6

Everyone laughs as Muddy hitches up her belt and, with a smile, fires back, "I can outride *you* any day."

Your uncle turns to the last cowhand. "And this is Earl. He's handy to have around when the beeves are stampeding."

You shake everybody's hands and follow Uncle Brad into the house. Inside, Aunt Lucy crushes you in a giant hug. "Why, you're just skin and bones! We're going to put some meat on you and show your mother just how to feed a growing child. I've got ham, rib eye steak, baked potatoes, pole beans, carrots, and a pumpkin pie for supper. Now, get cleaned up and we'll eat."

Uncle Brad shows you your room and leaves you to get ready for supper. The room has a large four-poster bed, an old beat-up dresser, and framed prints on the walls. Out the window you can see prairie and scrub brush for miles.

At the dinner table, you notice that places are set for four. Since Uncle Brad and Aunt Lucy have no children, you wonder who the fourth person could be.

Then the back door slams and a voice calls out, "Hey, Miss Lucy! What's for supper?"

Turn to page 10.

You maneuver around a half dozen more barrels and over some bales of hay, the last obstacle. The finish line is thirty feet ahead. You give the bay a swift kick, and she surges forward at a full gallop. You look over your shoulder. The other horse is about fifteen feet behind.

"We're going to win!" you yell in excitement.

"Yessssss!" Uncle Brad shouts.

But all at once your excitement is dashed. The bay comes to a sudden halt. You fly out of the saddle and over her head, onto the ground. You land on your back, stunned.

Turn to page 30.

8

It looks like you're going to get some veterinary experience sooner than you thought! There's just no time to get Walter. This calf is coming, and you're going to deliver it. You can see the calf's nose emerging already.

The heifer cries out in pain once more and pushes hard. You rub her belly and encourage her. It's the only thing you can think to do.

"Mooooooo!" she cries, straining to push.

The calf's head is out. It's covered with a thick, sticky fluid. It's really messy. The last thing you want to do is touch it.

The heifer pushes again, and more of the calf appears. Its front legs are out. Now the heifer rests for a few minutes to catch her breath. She looks exhausted. You're not sure if she has the strength to finish pushing the calf out. You have to help her now.

You grab the calf by its shoulders. You pull gently, helping the mother as she pushes. To your surprise, the calf comes out quickly. You cradle it in your arms as the heifer lays her head on the ground, totally spent.

The calf's hooves gently kick against your thighs. It twists to break free. You lay it on the ground beside its mother, where it hunts for her teat.

→

It's a beautiful moment, until you notice that you're covered with the same gunk as the calf. It's very sticky, and you need to wash up. You go back and get Rosie, and the two of you walk partway up the slope of the ridge to a stream you passed earlier. The stream is shallow this time of year. It rushes over the rocks of its bed in search of the larger creek down in the valley.

Rosie dips her head in the water to drink while you lie down in the stream with all your clothes on—including your boots. You let the cold, fresh water flow over you. Your shirt and pants quickly become heavy and drenched. Your boots fill up like buckets dipped into the stream. The chill sends shivers down your spine, but it feels good.

Turn to page 72.

10

"None of your business," Aunt Lucy calls back as she sets platters of steak and ham on the table. "Your job is to eat it, not know what it is."

There's a loud laugh from the kitchen. "Let me get cleaned up and I'll eat whatever is set in front of me."

A couple of minutes later, the person attached to the voice comes through the door from the kitchen. You're more than a little surprised. You were expecting a full-grown cowboy. Instead it's a scrawny little girl, a few inches shorter than you.

"This here is Natalie, Nat for short," Uncle Brad says, introducing the girl to you. "She's fourteen, just like you. She's living with us while her dad works out in the Escalante Desert for an oil company. She'll be with us the whole summer."

"You call me anything besides Nat, I'll tan your hide," she tells you.

You nod, not sure what to say.

"You two will be working together," Uncle Brad adds, "which reminds me. I've got a small change of plans." He leans on his elbows and gives you a serious look. "First, I need help rounding up those beeves on Hurricane Cliffs. We need to drive 'em down to Cedar City to sell. Walter, Earl, and Nat are heading out right after breakfast tomorrow." He glances at your aunt Lucy and winks.

"Get on with it, Brad," Aunt Lucy says.

Turn to page 12.

Uncle Brad takes a sip of his black coffee. "I've been elected president of this year's Cedar City Rodeo," he says proudly. "It's scheduled for the week after the drive. I'd appreciate a hand setting it up while the beeves are being driven to town."

You nod.

"Lastly, I need a steady hand here at the ranch to help Muddy break some mustangs Walter rounded up east of Snow Canyon." Uncle Brad smiles and rubs his chin. "Now, these are wild horses. The government sells them to us for two hundred dollars a head. They make the best cattle horses because they're not afraid of anything."

Turn to page 61.

You tell John Whittemore you'd like to ride Neutron, and he leads the bull into the chute as cowboys begin to collect along the top fence rail of the empty arena.

You pull your hat down over your forehead and climb to the top of the fence beside the chute.

"Well, here he is," John says to you. "Gentle as a lamb." The cowboys nearby laugh nervously.

"I don't know," you say. "He doesn't look so gentle." You stare at the bull's yellow eyes. He snorts and kicks the gate menacingly.

"Maybe this isn't such a good idea," you say, trying to back out gracefully.

"Aw, come on," John says. He points to a couple of cowboys standing in the ring. "Those fellas will protect you if you fall off."

You look over your shoulder to see if Uncle Brad is nearby. But he's not.

You take a deep breath. "Here goes nothing." You climb onto the back of the bull and lace your fingers around the rope attached to his back. That's all there is to hold on to.

Turn to page 23.

I'd like to help you track the strays," you tell Walter.

"All right. You'd better get some shut-eye now. Earl, you'll go with Nat and the chuck wagon tomorrow."

Everyone is tired, and you all settle into your bedrolls for an early night.

The next morning, Walter wakes you early. You wolf down a quick breakfast, and Walter says, "Time to saddle up. We'll head north and circle back to Earl and Nat with the herd day after tomorrow."

You nod and carry your saddle and blanket over to Rosie. After you lay the blanket on her back, you lift the saddle into place. You tighten the cinch. If the saddle is loose, it could slip right off, leaving you on the ground.

You fill your saddlebags with jerky, trail mix, and military surplus M.R.E.'s, which stands for "meals ready-to-eat." You tie down your bedroll and a rain slicker on the back of your saddle.

Walter points to a ridge on the horizon. "That's Missionary Ridge. It's about ten miles from here. We'll ride along the top of it. It'll give us a full view of the prairie."

You nod and fall in behind Walter.

$\longrightarrow$

By the time you reach the ridgetop, the sun has come up, but the sky has turned gray. A light chill fills the air.

"We're in for a storm," Walter says. "We better work fast."

Soon it starts to drizzle, and it becomes hard to see. A fog settles on the prairie, making it impossible to spot stray beeves.

"We're not going to find anything like this," you say.

Walter agrees. "We better find some shelter and wait it out." He spurs his horse down the side of the ridge. "There's an overhang down this way."

You and Walter quickly set up camp beneath the ledge. There's enough dry kindling around to start a fire.

Turn to page 83.

16

You hang on to the saddle horn for dear life as the bay bucks across the center of the corral. He fights furiously to throw you off, but you manage to keep your seat. Just when you think you're going to win, he throws his head up high and kicks his rear legs out. Your face smacks against his neck, and you fly out of the saddle.

Muddy is right there to pull the bay safely away so you're not stomped on.

You sit up, gingerly rubbing your nose. It's not bleeding, but it stings. You try to stand. You're dizzy, but you steady yourself enough to walk over to the corral fence.

Muddy has the bay cornered at the other end of the corral. She's pressing the horse against the fence to keep him from moving.

"Watch this!" Muddy shouts as she hops in the saddle.

Turn to page 92.

Walter waves you over. "Give me a hand with Nat."

The two of you lift Nat by the shoulders and drag her over to a rock. She slumps in exhaustion.

"We'll head out this afternoon to round up the herd," Walter explains. "Right now we need to clean up and get ready to move. I don't want to camp here another night and be sitting ducks for the wolves again."

You nod and start to stack the scattered cooking equipment out of the way of the chuck wagon so the team of horses can pull the wagon upright. As you're cleaning up, you decide that driving the chuck wagon wasn't so bad. In fact, it was a lot more comfortable than riding a horse all day. But if you volunteer to drive the chuck wagon, you'll be doing most of the cooking yourself, since Nat's hurt.

If you decide to volunteer to drive the chuck wagon, turn to page 100.

If you decide to keep your mouth shut and look for the runaway herd, turn to page 28.

Back at the camp, you grab a plate and ladle a large helping of rice and beans onto it. Then you spread butter on a hunk of corn bread and settle down against the trunk of an aspen to eat.

But as you sit down, Earl comes up and kicks your plate out of your hands.

"Hey!" you yelp, as beans drip onto your jeans.

"That's my place, rookie," Earl grumbles. "Get out!"

Before you know it, Walter is there. He grabs Earl by the arm. "If you touch any of my crew again, Earl, you're out of here."

Earl glares at Walter and then settles down next to a rock in the shadows, away from the campfire.

Walter hands you his napkin. "Don't pay Earl any mind. He's always tough on new cowhands." You both watch Earl shovel beans into his mouth. "I was thinking of having you and Nat handle the wagon. Earl's good at tracking stray cattle. It would keep him out of our hair for most of the trip."

You nod.

"Unless you and Nat *want* to chase down the strays." Walter takes a big bite of corn bread and chews it thoughtfully. "Either way, you won't have Earl in your face all the time. Which would you rather do— track strays down in Dutchman's Draw tomorrow, or take the chuck wagon ahead and set up the next night's camp with Nat?"

Turn to page 93.

Thoughts race through your mind about what to do. You know you can't fight Earl. He's twice your size. He'll pound you to a pulp.

Not taking your eyes off him, you slowly bend over to pick up your boots. As you grab your boots, you clutch a fistful of dirt in your other hand.

Then you make your move. You hurl the dirt into Earl's face and run as fast as you can toward the camp.

Earl takes off after you. At first he matches you stride for stride, and you're keeping a good twenty feet ahead of him. Then he begins to gain on you.

You glance over your shoulder and see him almost within arm's reach.

He reaches out and misses.

You struggle to run faster.

Earl reaches out again. This time he grabs a hunk of your hair and jerks you to a stop. He pulls your head back and balls his fist to punch you.

He lets his fist fly, but it's caught by another hand inches from your face.

"I don't think so, Earl," Walter says angrily. He has Earl's fist in his hand and is turning it backward.

Earl kneels from the pain. "Okay, okay, Walter. I wasn't going to hurt anybody."

→

"Not the way I see it," Walter says. He lets go of Earl's fist. Earl falls to the ground. "Get your gear and get out of here. You're fired!"

"Aw, c'mon, Walter," Earl pleads.

Walter shakes his head. "I don't want to see you around the Anchor P again."

Earl scrambles to his feet and heads for the camp.

"Get lost!" Walter yells after him. Then he turns to you. "You okay?"

You nod.

"Let's eat some supper, then." Walter turns and walks back to camp.

Turn to page 56.

You take a deep breath as Neutron becomes incredibly still.

John bends over and throws a handful of dirt into Neutron's face.

"Hey!" you shout, worried that this will make the bull mad.

But before you can say anything else, John opens the gate.

Neutron spins out and kicks his rear hooves high in the air. The back of your head smacks his rump. Your hat flies off, and you follow.

You sail high in the air. You feel weightless. Your legs are thrown way over your head. But the feeling lasts only a second. Then you slam hard into the dirt floor of the arena.

You experience excruciating pain, followed quickly by complete blackness.

All around you, cowboys jump over the fence and run toward you. The cowboys in the arena are working hard to distract Neutron.

But you don't see any of this. You're out cold.

Turn to page 44.

24

The horse bucks but not very convincingly. You smile and give her a kick in the flanks. You feel as if you're getting control. She lunges forward. You pull her head to the right with the reins, and she follows.

"You were right," Uncle Brad yells. "She's a gentle one."

You smile with satisfaction. Out of the corner of your eye you can see Uncle Brad helping Walter out of the corral.

You have a head start on the other horses. But the going is slow. The bay alternates between a gallop and a walk without warning, so you really have to fight to stay on.

You can hear the crowd laughing uproariously at the riders fighting their mounts. You know you must look silly flailing around on this bay. You can hear Uncle Brad's raucous laughter, too.

Your heart races as you round a barrel halfway through the obstacle course. You're in the lead and making good progress. The bay seems to be obeying you.

You take the bay over a low hurdle and through a small lake. You're still in the lead, but another rider is catching up. You're going to need a perfect ride from here to the end to win.

Turn to page 7.

Later in the day, the sun is riding low on the horizon as you drive the chuck wagon up a grassy knoll. For the last three hours, Nat has been whining and complaining next to you. Mostly, she has been going on and on about wolves. She seems to know everything about them. She says there used to be wolves all over the lower forty-eight states, but they were all killed off by ranchers. So the National Park Service reintroduced them in the West by bringing wolves down from Canada. Now the wolves are wandering out of the parks and killing cattle.

Nat keeps talking about what a pain the wolves are. You're surprised, since this is more than she has spoken in two days. "I wish they'd never brought 'em down. They're nothing but trouble."

Turn to page 90.

"Well, you hold the horse once I've roped it," Uncle Brad explains. "You see, we have to catch the horse, put a bridle and saddle on it, and then ride it. I'll do the roping and saddling, Walter will do the riding, and you can hold the horse steady for Walter so she doesn't throw the saddle off."

"No problem," you say. You're psyched for the competition.

"Walter's our best rider, so we've got a good chance in this race," Uncle Brad says.

"All you need to do is have a steady hand and don't let the horse spook you," Walter adds.

You and Uncle Brad watch the wild horses while you wait for the race event to be called. Both of you have opinions about which horse would be the best to catch. You're looking for a horse that's both gentle and fast.

A deep voice blows into the PA system by the stables. "Ahem. Contestants for the Wild Horse Race, please come to the judges' booth with your gear. The event will begin in five minutes."

"Let's go," Walter says.

You and about thirty others crowd around the judges' booth waiting for the signal to enter the arena. The horses are sent in first. They mill nervously about at the far end, away from the grandstand.

→

As you watch them, you realize that you're just as nervous as the horses, if not more so.

Red, white, and blue barrels are set up around the ring, along with a few low jumps. This is the obstacle course that Walter will have to maneuver. It looks as if it would be pretty easy—unless you're riding a horse that won't follow instructions.

Bang! A starter's pistol is fired.

Turn to page 84.

You tell Walter that you'd like to help him round up the rest of the herd.

"Well, that seems fair enough," he replies. "Earl, you can go with Nat in the wagon."

"This greenhorn ain't gonna be much help rounding up those beeves," Earl says to Walter, jerking his thumb in your direction.

"Earl, just do as I say. We're all taking turns with the chuck wagon, and now it's your turn," Walter tells him firmly. Earl grumbles but walks off and starts packing up camp.

Bending over to lift a cooler full of meat, you suddenly become faint and fall to your knees. You shake your head, trying to clear it, and abruptly feel nauseated. The wound on your forehead that you got when you fell last night has opened up. Bright red drops stain the ground before you.

Walter crouches beside you and asks, "Are you okay?"

"Yeah, just a little dizzy," you answer.

"Let's get that cut cleaned up." Walter grabs the first-aid kit.

Once the cut is cleaned and bandaged, Walter tells you, "You better head back to the ranch and have a doctor look at that."

→

You don't want to go back. "I'll be all right. I can have it looked at in Cedar City."

Walter shakes his head. "Your aunt would kill me if I let you wait that long to get it attended to. Nope. You're going back."

You kick the cooler in anger. The last thing you want to do is go back to the ranch. But Walter is the trail boss, and you have to do what he says.

"Besides," Walter adds, "Nat's ankle is really too twisted for her to make the trip. I need you to drive Nat on the chuck wagon back to the ranch. You can catch up to us at Windy Bluff in two days. Tell your uncle to bring supplies and meet us there."

Turn to page 68.

The rider behind you races past.

You shake your head, jump to your feet, and get back on your horse. You ride the bay across the finish line.

You win second place! Uncle Brad runs to your side and helps you down from the bay.

"All right!" you shout.

"How're you feeling?" Uncle Brad asks.

"A little dizzy," you answer, "but that's the best ride I ever had!"

The End

Walter slaps you on the back, and you cringe with pain. Your muscles are tied in knots from riding a horse over rough country for six hours. You don't know how you're going to survive if the pain doesn't let up.

"Let's get some grub," Nat suggests.

"Not just yet," Walter says. "I need you two to hobble the wagon's team over there by that grass." He points to a slope on the other side of Beaver Wash. You and Nat lead the horses over and tie up one front leg on each horse so they can't wander far.

Turn to page 19.

Then the emcee introduces the King and Queen of Cedar City Stampede Days. They ride around the ring on horses, waving to the crowd.

"You know," Uncle Brad says absentmindedly, "we need another person for the wild horse race."

"What's that?" you ask, hoping that Uncle Brad wants you to join the team.

Uncle Brad opens the Amateur Rodeo's schedule and shows you the page.

3:00 P.M.—Wild Horse Race
Three-person teams saddle an unbroken horse and ride it around an obstacle course.

"I could do this!" you shout.

Uncle Brad laughs. "Well, then, follow me. We've got work to do. The event's this afternoon."

You're out of your seat and halfway down the grandstand before Uncle Brad can stand up.

Walter meets you and Uncle Brad at the corral. Wild horses are milling about in a pack.

"Here, pin this to your back," Walter says, handing you the team's number. "I'm glad you're joining us. I don't know where Nat and Earl are. We got in from the trail last night. They said they would be here."

"Let's go through the routine," Uncle Brad says.

"What do I do?" you ask.

Turn to page 26.

You ride quickly and meet Walter about a mile down the ridge.

"What's up?" Walter asks, seeing the concern on your face.

As you explain about the heifer giving birth, he turns his horse and rides back down the ridge.

"Come on!" Walter shouts. "We don't have any time to spare."

You turn Rosie and gallop behind him. It doesn't take long to get back to the heifer.

But the moment you arrive, you know something's wrong.

Walter jumps off his horse and is on the ground next to the heifer in one quick movement.

He looks up at you and shakes his head. "She didn't make it. The calf got stuck, and she bled to death. She couldn't do it herself. She must have been too tired from the cattle drive and the stampede."

You nearly fall off your horse in shock. "I can't believe it—I only left her for a few minutes!"

"It's not your fault," Walter says. "This kind of thing happens."

You slide out of the saddle and kneel by the heifer. "Should I have stayed?"

→

"Honestly?" Walter replies. "It's hard to say. Sometimes you can help, and sometimes you can't."

You put your hand on the heifer's head. The animal is still warm. It surprises you how quickly and unexpectedly death can come.

You stand and shake your head in disbelief.

"Come on," Walter says softly. "We should get going. We're not going to find any strays in this brush."

Turn to page 46.

Back at the ranch, you and Muddy set to breaking horses right away. This time you save the paint for last and begin with the gentler horses.

The first horse Muddy saddles is a short and stumpy Appaloosa.

"Do you want the honors?" Muddy asks, holding the Appaloosa for you to climb on to.

"Sure," you answer. You hop off the fence and walk over to the horse.

The Appaloosa skitters away. Muddy pulls her back.

"I think she's a feral," Muddy says.

"What's that?"

"A horse that once belonged to somebody but then escaped and went wild. Yeah, the way she let me put the bit in her mouth tells me she's been ridden before." Muddy jerks the Appaloosa's head down to get her under control.

You climb on, expecting the horse to buck.

But she doesn't. Instead, she trots over to the fence and tries to rub you off by leaning her side into the rails.

You turn her head sharply with the reins. She spins around and gives a low kick. Not a real strong buck, just enough to let you know that she can do it if she wants to.

→

You give her a little kick in her flanks. She trots to the center of the corral.

"Not much to breaking this one," Muddy observes. "Take her around the corral a couple of times."

The Appaloosa neatly canters around the corral, only fighting back a little.

Unfortunately, the rest of the horses aren't so easy.

The next horse Muddy saddles is a sleek bay that shows a lot of spirit. He stomps his feet nervously as you try to climb into the saddle. The moment you're on, he pulls away from Muddy before she can hand you the reins.

Turn to page 16.

For some crazy reason you feel you have to ride one of these monsters.

"Do you think I could enter in the bull-riding comp?" you ask Uncle Brad.

"What, are you crazy?" Uncle Brad answers. "Bull riding is for the mentally deficient. My papa used to say bull riders wear size five hats because they haven't got much room for sense in their little heads." Uncle Brad walks away to lead some livestock into the stalls.

A tall old contractor who has overheard your conversation comes up. "You wanna ride a bull?"

"Yes," you answer.

"I'll show you how. It's not so hard." With a bowlegged gait, he leads you over to a stall where one of his bulls is stabled. "By the way, my name is John, John Whittemore."

You tell him your name and ask him what you have to do.

"All you have to do is stay on the bull for ten seconds," John says.

"That sounds easy," you answer.

➞

"It's the longest ten seconds you'll ever live if you can stay on." John grabs a bull-riding rig, which consists of two belts and a braided rope. He shows you how to wrap your fingers into the braid of the rope for a better grip. Then he explains that you have to ride up high on the bull's shoulders and pace your movements to the bull's.

"It's not as easy as it sounds," he says. "Normally, you'd practice your technique on a mechanical bull before you climbed up on a live one. But I'll tell you what. I'll let you take a practice ride on a bull of mine. His name is Neutron. I'm about to retire him because he's getting too old."

"Cool," you say. But then you have second thoughts. Uncle Brad's warning echoes in your mind. You're not sure whether you should give it a try or not. John tells you the bull is as gentle as a lamb. Can you trust him? You don't even know him.

If you decide not to ride, turn to page 52.

If you decide to ride the bull, turn to page 13.

"Wolves!" you shout. "Wolves!" You run as quickly as you can toward the others, shouting with each step. You're not sure if anyone can hear you because you've strayed so far from camp. You run harder, but you can't see where you're going. You catch your boot on something and fly face first to the ground.

You roll to your side and put your hand up to your face. It's wet and sticky with blood.

You hear the pounding of hooves and helpless cries of terror as the cattle race toward you. If you don't do something right away, you'll be trampled. You scurry on your hands and knees to a tree and quickly climb up into its branches.

By now, it's nearly daybreak. As you press yourself up against the tree, clinging to its branches for dear life, you feel the ground tremble.

Suddenly they are there. The beeves come flying right below you and your tree as they hurl themselves, panic-stricken, down into the gulch. There are more beeves than you could ever count pouring down the incline. Dust makes the air nearly unbreathable. You cover your face, but it still feels as if you're swallowing an entire desert.

Turn to page 60.

42

The sun is low over the horizon when you finally set up camp. You and the rest of the crew have been riding all day. You ate a lunch of beef jerky and dried apple slices in the saddle around noon. You haven't seen a steer, but Walter says not to expect to see one until tomorrow. The herd is in the hills fattening up on the spring grass.

The chuck wagon is parked among some aspen trees along a dry creek bed called Beaver Wash. Earl comes out from behind the wagon lugging a big steaming kettle.

"Chow time!" Walter shouts. He ties his horse to a nearby tree, giving him enough rope to graze on the surrounding grass.

You drop your saddle by the fire that Earl already has roaring and rub your back.

Turn to page 32.

After two days of busting broncos, you're getting tired of it and want a change of scenery. You wonder if Uncle Brad would send you to Cedar City to help out on the rodeo and debate with yourself about whether to ask. You know that if you do ask, Uncle Brad will probably let you go. But you're not sure if you should abandon Muddy. You'll be leaving her to finish the job of breaking the horses alone. Is that fair?

If you decide to stick around the Anchor P and work with Muddy, turn to page 70.

If you decide to ask Uncle Brad to let you go to Cedar City, turn to page 71.

44

You wake up in a hospital bed. Uncle Brad and two people you don't know are leaning over you. Their heads are silhouetted by bright lights behind them.

"How are you?" Uncle Brad asks gently.

You try to reply, but a wave of nausea cuts off your words.

"Don't speak," says a man in a white coat with a stethoscope around his neck. "Just rest. You took a bad spill."

"To say the least," Uncle Brad adds. "That was the dumbest thing I've ever seen someone do. Neutron is the most dangerous bull around. Most riders refuse to ride him when they get him in the draw."

"Huh?" you say, trying to sit up. "But John said—" You stop talking because an incredible throbbing shoots through your head.

"John is meaner than his bull," Uncle Brad explains. "He set you up."

You fall back into your bed and sleep.

The End

Muddy throws the saddle and gear onto the top rung of the fence. She climbs through the fence and widens the loop in her lariat. She clicks her tongue and swings the lariat over her head—once, twice, three times. On the upswing her hand releases the lariat. It flies high into the air, spinning toward the painted mustang.

As the lariat nears the mustang's head, you open the gate to enter the corral.

Seeing this, the mustang dips his head. The lariat passes over it and falls to the ground. The mustang whinnies and breaks for the open gate. At a flat-out gallop he butts the gate out of your hands. It swings wide open.

As if on cue, the other mustangs follow in a mad dash. Thundering across the corral, they bolt free before you can close the gate. They stream out of the yard and onto the prairie.

Turn to page 55.

46

The two of you ride toward the place where Walter thinks Nat and Earl will be camping that night. It's not easy finding them. Finally, though, Walter spots smoke from a fire drifting above a stand of pines.

"Over there." Walter points.

You nod and turn Rosie in that direction.

As you ride into camp, Earl yells, "What happened? You get lost? I thought we weren't meeting up for another day."

"We're not going to find any strays in that brush," Walter says.

"Humph," Earl snorts.

Nat is preparing supper. She hobbles around from the chuck wagon to the campfire pretty well, using her branch crutch.

You and Walter groom and feed the horses. Then you take a swim in a nearby stream. After your swim, you get out and change back into your clothes behind some bushes.

When you come out of the bushes looking for your boots, Earl is standing there, waiting for you. He looks angry.

"Hey, Earl."

"Hey yourself, greenhorn," Earl says nastily. "You cost me some hard-earned money today."

"What do you mean?" you ask.

→

"That heifer you killed today. And her calf," Earl says. He spits. "I'm working for a percentage. Every heifer we lose costs me money. Money that's gonna get me through the winter."

"It wasn't my fault—" you start to say, but Earl interrupts, kicking your boots toward you.

"Put on your boots. I'm going to teach you a lesson about driving cattle," he growls. He balls up his fists and rolls his massive shoulders.

Turn to page 20.

Uncle Brad spurs his horse forward, swinging his lariat high over his head, as the horses come charging.

You hold back about twenty feet and spin your lariat at your side.

The paint roars up the slope. Uncle Brad releases his rope. It flies through the air in a perfect, arcing loop. It's aimed right on target.

But the paint pulls up, and the loop falls short.

Smart fella, you think as you get ready for your try.

You give your rope one more hard swing and let it fly. It soars straight at the paint.

Again the paint pulls up, but this time it doesn't work. Your loop slips right over his head.

Quickly you pull your rope taut and wrap it around your saddle horn. The paint jerks hard, but Rosie can fight it. If you hadn't tied the rope to the horn, you'd be on the ground right now. The paint would have easily ripped you out of the saddle.

"Good roping!" Muddy says. She slaps you on the back.

"Let's rope the rest of the horses and head back to the ranch," Uncle Brad says.

Muddy and Uncle Brad ready their ropes and catch the rest of the horses easily. The herd stops fighting once its leader is caught.

Turn to page 36.

50

You decide to help Muddy bust the mustangs. After breakfast the following morning, you meet her by the corral.

"First of all, this isn't some camp for city slickers," Muddy tells you gruffly. "This is a ranch, and we've got work to do, so don't think it's gonna be all fun and games."

"Yes ma'am!" You smile. Muddy sounds tough, but you can tell she has a kind heart.

You can't wait to climb on the back of a wild mustang. It seems like the ultimate battle between human and beast. You're primed to find out if you can turn a wild, bucking mustang into a good saddle horse.

In the corral a dozen horses are milling around nervously. They are mostly bays, but one painted horse catches your eye. He's circling the pack as if he's herding them. He holds his head up high as he prances and snorts.

"Let's get to work," Muddy calls as she walks up with a saddle, a blanket, and a bit. "I figure we could break two or three today, two or three tomorrow, and so on until we're done."

"Only two or three?" You're surprised. You thought you'd do them all today.

Muddy smiles. "You'll see. Mustangs are a pretty stubborn lot. It's going to take a while."

Turn to page 45.

You, Nat, and Walter saddle up. Earl sits like a king on the wagon's bench. Together you ride from the ranch toward a cluster of brownish green hills to the east. Beyond them tower the majestic Rocky Mountains.

You point to the hills. "Is that where we're going?"

"Yup," Walter says. "That's Hurricane Cliffs. You'll like it. Some of the prettiest country I've ever seen."

"Why do they call it Hurricane Cliffs?" you ask.

"Because at night up there the wind howls so fierce you'd think it's a hurricane come to carry you off," Walter says.

"Let's get moving," Earl shouts back at you. "We've got twenty miles to cover before setting up camp." He drives the wagon on ahead, with everyone else following.

Dust from the wagon's wheels blows in your face, and you begin to cough.

"Better cover your mouth and nose with a bandanna," Nat advises. "Dust is a fact of life out here."

Turn to page 42.

You pass on the chance to ride the bull. You spend a few days helping Uncle Brad. Then the rodeo begins. You walk into the stands with a bag of peanuts to watch the bull-riding event. Secretly, you half wish you had ridden that bull.

The rodeo emcee announces the bull-riding event over the PA system. "This here bull has got more than a little Western in him. The last cowboy to ride him broke his neck. Tonight will be Neutron's last time out of the gate. His owner, John Whittemore, is retiring him to the stud farm. I don't envy the cowboy who draws one of Neutron's offspring. I'm sure he'll be a chip off the old atom. Heh, heh, heh!"

The crowd erupts in laughter and claps as the bell clangs for the gate to open.

Neutron? That was the bull you were going to ride a couple of days ago. Now you realize you were being set up. You're glad you didn't bite.

Neutron spins out of the chute. His rider hangs on for dear life, a look of panic on his face. Suddenly Neutron stops in the middle of the ring. The crowd becomes quiet. The bull kicks his rear hooves high into the air and twists his head almost completely around. The cowboy on his back goes sailing in the opposite direction.

→

Quickly the rodeo clowns run to the rider's aid. One distracts the bull while the other helps the rider to his feet and out of the ring.

"Five point two seconds!" the rodeo emcee announces. "Not long enough to score."

The audience groans in disappointment.

Just then, you spot Uncle Brad coming up into the stands. You wave him over.

"Enjoying the show?" Uncle Brad asks.

"You bet," you say. "Those bulls are pretty mean."

"The meanest," Uncle Brad says. He takes his Stetson off and wipes his brow with his handkerchief.

Turn to page 33.

54

"Hey, Nat, what's for supper? How's your leg? Any trouble on the trail?" Earl peppers Nat with questions but ignores you.

All the attention seems to mellow Nat out. By the time supper is ready, she's laughing and swapping stories.

You're feeling pretty good yourself. You've just made your first camp supper, a bean and venison stew. As you ladle it out onto plates, everyone remarks on how good it smells.

The howling of the wind all night long makes it hard to sleep. You can't keep what happened with the wolves the day before out of your mind, and you wonder if somehow you led the wolves to the herd.

Turn to page 58.

Moments later, the dust is settling and the ranch is
oddly quiet.

This lasts only a second, however, because Muddy
starts screaming at you. "Never! I mean *never*! *Never*
open the gate to a corral unless you're bringing an animal in or taking one out!"

You try to apologize but are cut off.

Muddy throws her hat on the ground and stomps on
it. "Now we've got to get those horses back. Only it's
gonna be twice as hard because they know what's waiting for them when they're caught." She kicks the dirt
and picks up her hat, then screws it back onto her
head.

"I'm going to get my horse," she says.

Turn to page 80.

56

When you get back to camp, Earl has already left. Nobody says a word about what happened. You eat supper as Nat and Walter swap stories about past cattle drives. When the moon is well overhead, Walter puts out the fire and you climb into your bedroll for a good night's sleep.

You hear Walter singing a ballad as you drift off.

> *The winds may blow*
> *And the thunder growl.*
> *A cowboy's life*
> *Is a royal life,*
> *His saddle his kingly throne.*

The End

Uncle Brad waves Muddy to circle around the horses while you and he get your lariats ready. You watch Muddy follow the slope of the rise around the meadow. As Muddy comes up behind the mustangs, the paint raises his head, sniffing the air. Suddenly he whinnies and kicks his forelegs up. In one swooping motion the horses break into a gallop, headed directly at you and Uncle Brad.

"Go for the paint," Uncle Brad says. "He's the leader. If we catch him, the other horses will follow."

Turn to page 49.

58

Arrooooooo! Arrooooooo!

A wolf's cry echoes through the night. It cuts through the whistling wind and calls you out of your bedroll. You saddle Rosie and follow the wolf's cries. You ride until daybreak. When dawn arrives, you find yourself in a deep wash littered with branches and brush. Your limbs are heavy from lack of sleep as you follow the path that the spring rains and melting snow have gouged out of the earth.

Rosie warns you long before you see him. The wolf is sleeping curled up against the wall of the wash. As Rosie nervously stamps her foot and tries to back away, the wolf awakens.

You and the wolf lock eyes. His yellow eyes bore into yours. Your heart slams in your chest like an animal caught in a trap. As slowly as possible, you back Rosie down the wash, trying not to disturb the wolf or spook Rosie.

You realize that the wolf is after your uncle's herd. Somehow you've got to stop this wolf—and the rest of his pack—from raiding the herd as well.

Turn to page 75.

60

Before long the herd has passed you. You climb down from the tree. You brush the dirt from your clothes and try to cough up some of the dust you swallowed.

Walter comes riding up to you. "We thought you'd been trampled when we couldn't find you at the camp."

"Well, I almost was," you answer shakily. "It was wolves."

"I know." Walter nods. "They got themselves a nice fat steer for breakfast. I saw them dragging it off as I chased the herd. And I counted ten other dead steers that they left behind."

Back at camp, Earl is taping a splint on Nat's leg. The stampede came right through camp, and it looks like it, too. The tents are nothing but rags now, and the chuck wagon is turned on its side. The team of horses is nowhere in sight.

Turn to page 18.

You've had your heart set on riding the range with real cowboys and rounding up cattle. But being behind the scenes of a rodeo might be too exciting to pass up. And you'd like to try busting mustangs, too, especially since horses are your favorite animals. It's a tough decision.

If you want to go on the cattle drive,
turn to page 78.

If you decide to bust some broncs,
turn to page 50.

If you want to go behind the scenes of a real
rodeo, turn to page 71.

You ride up and slap the heifer on her rump.

"Moooo!" she cries in protest, and stands her ground.

You circle her and prod her with the toe of your boot one more time, but she still won't budge. You grab a lariat off the horn of your saddle and loop it around her neck.

You click your tongue and give Rosie a little kick. Rosie trots forward, the slack rope tightens, and the heifer digs her hooves into the earth. Rosie moos and stops.

Awkwardly, you slide out of the saddle and march back to the heifer. She has plopped down in the grass on her side. As she lies there, she kicks her legs in the air.

"Mooooooo!" she cries, and kicks the air faster.

"Please don't go into labor, Bessie," you say nervously. You scan the edge of the ridge for Walter, but he is nowhere in sight. You walk back to Rosie and loosen the rope from around the saddle horn. It falls slack on the ground. You tie Rosie's reins to a tree and walk back.

"Mooooo!" the heifer cries again. This time it sounds as if she's in pain.

⟶

You rub her stomach. The stiff brown fur bristles against your hand. Then you feel something strange. At first you're not sure what it is. But when it happens again, you're certain that it's a kick from inside her belly.

"Oh, no!" you gasp, realizing that the heifer *is* about to birth a calf. You back away from her as if she were a bomb ready to explode. "Not that! I can't deliver a calf."

You have no idea what to do. You want to ride and catch up to Walter. He'll know what to do. But you also know that this heifer might need help delivering her calf—right away.

If you decide to stay with the heifer and wait for Walter to double back, turn to page 8.

If you decide to ride ahead to catch Walter, turn to page 34.

64

You climb the trellis nailed to the side of the house and scramble onto the roof. Aunt Lucy hands you the hose. You soak the roof with water. Meanwhile, Aunt Lucy grabs another hose and sprays the front porch.

From the roof you can see the entire ranch. Muddy is frantically trying to herd the horses into the corral. Uncle Brad is still trying to get all the horses out of the barn. There are thirty horses and only about half are out.

Suddenly there's a loud crash. The barn entrance has collapsed. Uncle Brad is nowhere to be seen. He's trapped in the barn!

Before Muddy or Aunt Lucy notice what has happened, you've slid down a drainpipe and run toward a window in the side of the barn. You pick up a rock and smash the window open.

"Uncle Brad," you scream. "Uncle Brad! You can get out here!"

There's no answer.

Turn to page 77.

66

You choose the chuck wagon for tomorrow.

"Hey, Sleeping Beauty, time to start peeling potatoes," Nat whispers in your ear.

You brush the words away as if they were a pesky fly.

There's a pause. The quiet murmur of crickets fills the night air again.

Then . . . *"Get up!"* Nat screams in your ear.

You sit bolt upright in your bedroll. "Whaa? Whaa?" You blink and try to focus. "It's still dark out," you complain, curling back up in your bedroll.

Nat rips the blankets off. "We've got to have breakfast ready at dawn. And that means peeling potatoes at four A.M." Nat tosses a potato and the peeler in your lap. She looks like she's enjoying this a bit too much.

You groan. "Maybe being in the saddle all day wouldn't be so bad after all."

"It's too late to change your mind," Nat says. "Let's get moving."

You and Nat prepare breakfast and load the chuck wagon with the trail gear. Earl and Walter pack their lunches in their saddlebags and ride up into Hurricane Cliffs. You and Nat start out on the dry, dusty trail to the next campsite.

$\longrightarrow$

Late in the morning, a boom echoes across the hills. The ground shakes, knocking pots and pans from their hooks.

"Earthquake!" you scream as you cover your head.

Nat breaks into uncontrollable laughter. "That isn't any earthquake. That's just somebody drilling for oil. I'll show you." She turns the wagon off the track. "I bet they're over in this gulch."

Over the crest of a hill you see a big gray truck with cables running out of its back end. A huge drill is churning up soil. Then the drill is pulled from the ground, and someone drops something down into the hole it created. Suddenly there's another loud boom, and the ground shakes again.

"What's that?" you ask.

Turn to page 97.

Reluctantly, you do as Walter asks. By the time Earl and Walter return to camp with the herd, you're ready to head back. The chuck wagon is hitched to the team and Nat is sitting next to you on the buckboard.

Earl and Walter wave as you roll out of sight.

When the Anchor P comes into sight, you see Uncle Brad sitting on the corral fence. He's watching Muddy ride an ornery-looking mustang. The horse bucks and turns with amazing speed.

Uncle Brad runs over to the wagon as you pull up. He looks at you and Nat with concern. "What happened?"

Nat lifts her hurt ankle. "Stampede. The wagon fell on my ankle. Walter insisted I get it looked at, but I could've finished the drive."

You don't get a chance to tell Uncle Brad about your head injury because Muddy interrupts. "Maybe you should give this mustang a ride. I'm too beat up to get on another horse today."

You nod and try to contain your excitement. You pull your hat down low on your head, hoping Uncle Brad won't notice the bandage.

→

Uncle Brad examines Nat's ankle, which is wrapped up tight in a bandage. "Muddy, would you ask Lucy to call Doc Wiggins and tell him we'll meet him at his office right away?"

Muddy runs to the house while your uncle helps Nat down from the wagon and into the truck. Nat grimaces with pain. It's obvious that her ankle is much worse than she'll admit.

Turn to page 101.

70

That night you dream about busting broncos.
Clang! Clang! Clang!

You sit bolt upright in your bed. It's the middle of the night. The noise is deafening. You scramble from under the blankets and hurry to the window.

Over by the bunkhouse, Muddy is furiously clanging the dinner bell. She's bathed in a deep, red-yellow glow, a light unlike anything you've seen before. You turn your head to see where it's coming from and gasp.

The barn is on fire!

Without hesitating, you pull on your clothes and run barefoot into the yard.

Uncle Brad is running to the barn with a bucket of water. "We've got to get the horses out!"

He throws the water on a horse blanket, wraps it around his body, and runs into the barn. Flames lick the roof and shoot out of the hayloft.

Turn to page 74.

You tell Uncle Brad you want to work on the rodeo. As you expected, he says you can go ahead.

The next day you arrive at the Cedar City fairgrounds. The acres of parking lots are empty. It feels strange driving in.

"We're going over here," Uncle Brad says, "behind the stockyard." He pulls the truck up next to a long cattle transport.

The intense smell of livestock just about knocks you over as you climb out of the cab. There's a big hand-painted sign over the entrance to the rodeo grounds.

NOT RESPONSIBLE FOR INJURIES!

You swallow nervously. Obviously, bareback bronc and bull riding aren't for the faint of heart.

Uncle Brad sees you staring at the sign and laughs. "That's so the cowboys know they have to pay for their own broken arms and legs and backs and heads. Some of them aren't too smart. They need to be reminded."

Turn to page 76.

You lie in the water for a while, then climb out of the stream and undress. You squeeze as much excess water as you can from your clothes, then hang them to dry in the sunlight on a nearby tree limb.

Once your clothes are mostly dry, you dress and ride Rosie back to the mother and her calf. They haven't moved, though the calf is already clumsily trying to stand.

The calf's long, spindly legs press down unsteadily as its hooves paw the earth. First it gets its front end upright. Then it's almost on its hind legs when its front legs collapse, and the calf rolls onto its back. It's a funny, sweet sight.

You hobble Rosie to let her graze, and you set up camp. The calf and heifer will need to rest before they can travel, so you decide to wait with them. You know Walter will circle back once he sees you're not keeping pace with him.

You can't wait until he returns. He won't believe what you've just done. "Nobody will," you say, shaking your head.

The End

Horses begin to gallop wildly out of the barn. Uncle Brad must have gotten in and opened all the stalls up. Soon a dozen horses are sprinting in terror around the ranch.

You run for the garden hose in the toolshed and hook it up to a faucet near the corral and barn. As you coat the sides of the barn with water, you realize how pointless your efforts are.

Aunt Lucy runs from the house and grabs you by the arm. "The barn is lost," she yells. "Spray the water on the roof of the house so the fire won't spread to it." Her voice sounds desperate. "We don't want to lose that, too!"

Turn to page 64.

As you round a bend in the wash, out of the wolf's sight, you get an idea. You spur Rosie up the side of the wash. Then you climb down and tie her to a young birch a hundred feet away. You tie one end of a rope to a sturdy tree next to the wash and inch your way along the top edge, holding the rope's loose end.

When you come to the place where the wolf is resting, you stop and make a loop in your rope. You lean over the edge and look down. Just below you, the nose of the wolf is visible.

Slowly and quietly, you drop the loop down in front of the wolf's nose. But before you can get a good grip on the rope, the wolf lunges from his den. His head slips through the loop and pulls the rope right out of your hands. Luckily you think to stomp on the coil of rope on the ground beside you. You see the wolf yanked backward as the rope goes taut. He bares his teeth and growls viciously.

After reaching down and getting a good grip on the rope, you quickly wrap the end around the tree. The wolf growls as his huge neck muscles flex and tighten, keeping the rope from strangling him. You need to get out of here quickly. You have no idea how long the rope will hold against the wolf's struggles.

Turn to page 81.

You laugh and follow Uncle Brad to the stables.

"We've got to clean these stables out before tomorrow when the bronc and bull contractors arrive with their livestock," Uncle Brad explains. "You grab that rake, and I'll work this shovel."

Together you and Uncle Brad fill and cart fifty wheelbarrows of manure and soiled hay out of the stable. Then you spread fresh hay in each stall and fill the watering troughs. You're done by dinnertime.

"Where do we eat?" you ask Uncle Brad.

"The Cactus Cafe has a great band tonight and huge steaks." You drive to the edge of town and park in a big lot beside a lone building that looks like a barn.

Inside, you find seats near the stage and order massive steaks.

When your plates arrive, the featured band, Pioneer Heaven, has started its first song. It's an Old West camp song called "Kansas Line."

Turn to page 98.

You spot Uncle Brad's boot sticking out of one of the stalls. You climb in through the window. Uncle Brad is still conscious. He's just had the wind knocked out of him. You help him up, and he leans on you as you both hurry back to the window.

The intense heat almost makes you faint. Your eyes tear up from the smoke. The air is getting too hot to breathe. But you make it to the window and push Uncle Brad out into the yard. You follow and collapse to the ground, gasping for air.

The sound of the barn caving in on itself is the last thing you hear as you pass out.

Turn to page 103.

You decide that rounding up cattle is the job for you.

Cock-a-doodle-doo! The crow of a rooster wakes you at dawn. You pull on the jeans, work shirt, and boots your parents bought you before you left. Then you head down to the kitchen.

Breakfast is already set out. A platter of sausage patties, bacon, and eggs commands the center of the table, along with a tower of buttered toast. Aunt Lucy has poured you and Nat big glasses of orange juice and is now pouring coffee for Uncle Brad and herself.

Uncle Brad looks at you seriously. "You've never been on a cattle drive before, so I want you to stick close to Nat. She'll show you the ropes."

Nat nods in agreement.

"Sure thing, Uncle Brad," you answer, piling scrambled eggs on your plate. You never eat breakfast like this at home. Your mom is always worried about the fat in bacon and the cholesterol in eggs.

After breakfast you and Nat walk out to the bunkhouse to load the gear for the cattle drive onto the chuck wagon. There's a storeroom in the bunkhouse where all the pots, pans, sacks of flour, and other staples are kept.

→

"Hey, there!" Muddy calls to you and Nat. She's sitting in a chair on the bunkhouse porch sipping coffee. "I'm glad you're working the cattle drive. That means I get to stay at the ranch to break those mustangs."

"I'm glad, too," Earl says sarcastically as he pulls up with the chuck wagon. "I'm tired of looking at that mangy face of yours. My eyes need a rest."

The chuck wagon looks as if it just rode out of an old movie.

"Why don't we have a four-wheel-drive truck? Wouldn't that be easier than a wagon?" you ask Nat.

"Not really," Nat answers. "You have to have gas for a truck. Horses just need grass. And trucks, even four-wheel-drive ones, get stuck. A wagon can be pulled almost anywhere if you've got a good team of horses."

"Get off your rumps and let's get going," Earl yells.

Turn to page 51.

80

"Hold on there!" Uncle Brad calls out from the porch. He walks over to the corral as Muddy comes back from the stables, leading her horse and fuming.

"I saw it all and it wasn't anybody's fault," Uncle Brad says. "These things happen."

"Well, Walter isn't going to understand when he gets back and we tell him we lost those horses," Muddy counters.

"No, he won't be too pleased," Uncle Brad says thoughtfully. He pats you on the back encouragingly. "But we can round 'em up again. They can't have got too far. And they sure as shootin' left one big trail for us to follow."

Muddy nods, still looking upset.

"Let's saddle up and bring 'em back," Uncle Brad says.

Turn to page 88.

You run back to Rosie, jump in the saddle, and return at a gallop to camp. Everyone is awake.

"Where have you been?" Walter asks.

"Yeah," Earl puts in. "You been stirring up the wolves again?"

You shake your head, catch your breath, and tell your story. "I caught a wolf in a wash about two miles to the west. I thought we should tell the Park Service so they can bring him back to the park."

"Forget that!" Nat barks. "Let's shoot him while we have the chance."

Turn to page 86.

You pass the afternoon in easy conversation. Walter tells you that he studied to be a park ranger but got sidetracked by ranching. He tells you about hiking and camping throughout this part of the state with his father. He's been over every inch of this area five or six times.

You tell Walter about your dream to become a doctor or a veterinarian. You tell him about your pets: how your beagle loves to chase pigeons in the park, the way your tabby cat tortures your dog, and your two pythons.

After a meal of beef stew M.R.E., you both climb into your bedrolls for sleep. The rain is beginning to let up, and the clouds are moving off. It looks as if tomorrow will be clear.

Turn to page 87.

"That's it! Let's go!" Uncle Brad yells. The gate to the arena opens, and the three of you run after the horses.

It's total mayhem. As the contestants rush toward the horses, the horses panic and dash randomly around the arena.

With a lariat swinging wildly overhead, Uncle Brad runs after the bay that you both chose as the gentlest. You try to cut the bay off from the other side while Walter follows with the saddle and reins.

Uncle Brad snares the bay on his first try. All around you other contestants are crazily going after horses. A few are attempting to saddle their horses, but most are still trying to catch one.

Walter throws the blanket and saddle onto the bay's back. Uncle Brad hands you the rope.

"Pull her head down so I can get the bridle on," Uncle Brad says.

You bring the bay's head down and lock her neck under your arm.

The bay is now spinning in circles as Walter tries to strap on the saddle. Uncle Brad cinches the bridle tight and turns to help Walter.

Suddenly Walter loses his balance, just as he cinches the saddle under the horse's belly. The horse jumps and lands smack on Walter's leg.

→

"Agggghhh!" Walter screams in pain. He rolls to the edge of the corral to get out of the way of the horses.

Uncle Brad runs to Walter. You hop on the horse without a second thought.

The bay takes off! Only she goes sideways, right into the fence. She smashes your leg against the rail.

You yelp in pain but hang on. You grab the reins and pull her away from the fence.

Turn to page 24.

"Put that thought out of your mind, Nat," Walter shouts angrily. "There's a ranger station about fifteen miles to the south. They'll take care of the wolf." He turns to you and says, "Would you mind riding to the ranger station and showing them where the wolf is while we move the herd on?"

"No problem," you answer.

Everyone dumps their coffee on the fire and quickly begins to pack up their gear.

Earl slaps Nat on the back and says with a big grin, "Looks like you're on your own. You think you can handle it?"

"If you don't shut up, you'll get no supper," Nat growls sourly.

You ride quickly to the ranger station, where the rangers respond to your news with relief.

"We've been tracking that fella for weeks," a tall, burly ranger says. "Let's go get him, Brad."

Brad, a wiry man in a green ranger uniform, nods and opens a gun cabinet.

"You're not going to kill him, are you?" you ask in surprise.

Turn to page 94.

The next morning you and Walter are in the saddle early. You climb back up the ridge and follow it north. The wet clay makes the going slow. You slog along the muddy trail for what seems like hours before you spy a beef.

Below and to your left, under a stand of aspen trees, stands a massive heifer grazing on prairie grass. You turn Rosie down the side of the ridge toward the heifer, while Walter continues along the upper ridge.

"I'll ride parallel to you down at the bottom with this one," you call over your shoulder.

"Good idea," Walter says. "I'll point out others as we go along."

You weave around some brush and lead Rosie down the steep slope. When you get to the heifer, you notice that her midsection is unusually large. Either she's been fattening up on prairie grass all spring, or she's pregnant. You're glad you found her, because you know that either way she'll fetch a great price at the cattle auction.

Turn to page 62.

You and Uncle Brad hurry into the barn and saddle your horses. Soon the three of you are following the mustangs. The prairie where they ran is so torn up by their hooves that it's easy to track them.

You're pretty upset, no matter what Uncle Brad says. "This is all my fault," you tell him.

Uncle Brad laughs. "Don't let Muddy bother you. Wait till I remind her of Wilken's Bluff at supper tonight. She ran fifty head of cattle off a cliff. Losing these mustangs is a nuisance, but it's not fatal. The ranch won't go under because of it."

You feel a little better, but not much. You ride on in silence.

You're the first to spot the mustangs. About two miles from the ranch, you come to the top of a rise. Below, in the middle of an expanse of grass, the mustangs are grazing.

You raise your hand to stop Uncle Brad and Muddy. Then you point toward the mustangs, making sure not to spook them.

Turn to page 57.

Walter comes in about half an hour after Earl.

"What took you so long?" Earl asks irritably. "I wanted to eat and these two trail rookies here wouldn't let go of that grub till you came in."

"I just wanted to make sure the herd was relaxed," Walter says. "I saw some wolf tracks out in that gully, and I don't want any trouble tonight. We put the herd south of the camp so the wolves will have to come by us to get to them."

You eat a hearty dinner by firelight as the sky darkens. When the moon rises, it's only a sliver; it looks like a fingernail clipping. The sky is cloudless and the stars shine so brightly that you could almost read by their light. But you're too tired to read. This has been another long day, and you quickly fall asleep once your head hits your bedroll.

Turn to page 95.

You nod absently, mentally making a note to yourself never to talk about wolves in front of Nat again. You're not so sure Nat is right, especially when you remember what Walter said earlier this morning—"This is their home, not ours."

Suddenly Nat jerks the reins from your hands.

"Pull the wagon to the right!" she yells. "Don't let the horses see that stream. They'll make a dash for it, and you won't be able to get them away."

Nat pulls hard on the reins, but the horses have seen the water. They ignore her insistent yank and trot casually down the slope.

"Sorry, Nat," you say. You don't know what's gotten into her. She's become awfully cranky since she sprained her ankle.

"Well, then, we might as well camp here," Nat says. "It's as good a place as any. And it should protect us from the winds tonight."

"Winds?" you ask.

"I can smell 'em." Nat sniffs. "They're coming from the southwest. They're the winds that give Hurricane Cliffs its name."

The chuck wagon comes to a stop at the stream, and the horses dip their mouths into the cool water.

→

It doesn't take long to get a fire going and unload the essentials. Nat isn't much help. She sits on a wooden crate like a queen, giving directions. "Put that cook pot over here. Get some kindling before it gets dark. Cover these beans with water. Where's the cornmeal?"

After a while, Nat ends up back on her subject of the day: wolves. "If you catch a wolf, park rangers come and pick it up and drive it back to the park. A lot of good that does, though. In a week they're back, looking for cattle to eat."

Just when you've heard all you can stand from Nat, the sour smell of cattle tells you that the rest of the crew is near. Earl is the first to arrive at the campsite.

Turn to page 54.

The bay immediately breaks for the center of the corral and tries the same trick. Muddy is ready, however, and turns the horse's head away. She rides the horse until he's exhausted.

"Way to ride!" you shout, impressed. She is obviously an expert bronc buster.

Muddy dismounts, takes off the saddle, and puts it on a mottled gray horse.

You are mesmerized by Muddy's skill and grace. The horse breaks quickly. By the end of the day, half the mustangs have been ridden.

Together you and Muddy store the gear back in the stable for the night.

"We'll have to ride them again tomorrow," Muddy explains. "They'll be just as ornery tomorrow as they were today. It'll take a couple of days' riding to break them completely." Muddy slaps you on the back. "Good job today. You rode 'em like a pro."

"Thanks," you say, knowing that Muddy is being generous with her compliments.

"Let's get some grub," she says.

Turn to page 43.

"Which would *you* rather do?" you ask Nat.

"Doesn't matter to me," she says. "I've done both already."

"If I take the wagon, can I ride with the herd the next night?" you ask Walter.

"Sure," he says. "I figure everyone should take a turn with the wagon."

You rub your back. It's pretty stiff. You're not used to spending so much time in the saddle. Maybe it would be a good idea to work your way into it a little more slowly. On the other hand, you know from experience that if you don't keep your muscles loose, it could be even harder to keep riding.

If you decide to ride with Nat in the chuck wagon,
turn to page 66.

If you decide to track strays,
turn to page 14.

"Naw," Brad says. "We've got a couple of tranquilizer guns in here. We'll just put him to sleep so we can carry him back to the park and set him free again. You ready, Rick?"

"Yep," Rick answers, heading for the door. "Why don't you wait here and we'll take you back to the Anchor P on the way to the park?"

"Thanks," you say.

"We got some videos in the back room," Brad says. "We should be back in a few hours."

After the two rangers leave, you settle onto the couch in the back room, turn on a John Wayne movie, and immediately fall asleep. You haven't had a good night's sleep since you left the ranch, and the cushions on the old couch are just too comfortable.

The End

At some point in the night, a far-off howl wakes you. *Arrooooooo! Arrooooooo!*

You're not sure what it is, but you're drawn to it. You climb out of your bedroll and wander beyond the light of the campfire. When you pass the horses, they whicker softly. The dirt and dry grass beneath your feet crunch almost like snow. You climb to the top of a crest that gives you a view of the herd of cattle in the distance.

Arrrrooooo! Arrrooooooo!

"Wolves," you whisper under your breath. Their dark, shadowy shapes prowl along the crest opposite you, about a hundred yards away.

Suddenly the wolves begin to run. You try to count them but can't make out more than four or five. The cool, crisp night air makes it easy to see the white puffs of breath from their mouths as they leap and play. You watch as they move down the valley toward the dry streambed—toward the camp and toward the herd.

Turn to page 41.

"Dynamite," Nat answers. "Those things spread out along the cable are called geophones. They listen for the charge of the dynamite echoing through the earth. That tells them where an oil pocket might be located. My dad's working with another crew about four hundred miles north in the Escalante Desert, doing the same thing."

You get back on the trail, and by midafternoon Nat recommends setting up camp. "Walter and Earl won't get much further than this by nightfall," she says. "We'd better wait for them down by those junipers."

You notice the dry bed of a creek as you head for the trees. Two sets of tracks follow alongside the creek bed. You point to them.

"Wolves," Nat says. "The government reintroduced them to the parks a few years ago. They're a real nuisance. They spook the horses and beeves."

Turn to page 102.

The band is great, and you enjoy hearing the old cowboy song.

Come all you jolly cowmen, don't you want to go
Way up on the Kansas Line?
Where you whoop up the cattle from morning till night
All out in the midnight rain.

I've been where the lightnin', the lightnin' tangled in my
  eyes,
The cattle I could scarcely hold;
Think I heard my boss man say:
"I want all brave-hearted men who ain't afraid to die
To whoop up the cattle from morning till night,
Way up on the Kansas Line."

The cowboy's life is a dreadful life,
He's driven through heat and cold;
I'm almost frozen with the water on my clothes,
A-ridin' through heat and cold.

The next morning you're at the fairgrounds early. The livestock contractors are lining up to unload their bulls and broncs.

→

You watch the bulls being off-loaded. They're the meanest-looking animals you've ever seen. Most of the bulls are Brahmans. Ranchers began importing Brahman bulls from India more than a century ago. You're mesmerized by the massive humps rising like mountains from the backs of their necks, by their gray, slickhaired hides, and by their bad tempers. They look *mean*.

Turn to page 38.

100

Once you've cleaned up the campsite, everyone gathers around the campfire to rest. You tell Walter and Nat that you'd like to stick with Nat and chuck wagon duty.

"Fine with me," Walter says.

"Thanks," Nat says. "I'll show you how to drive the chuck wagon. It's easy."

The air is dense with woodsmoke and the smell of burning coffee. Walter and Earl have their hands wrapped around steaming mugs. Your hands are buried deep in your jean jacket pockets, while Nat's are cupped before her mouth as she breathes warm air into them.

Walter sighs. "Those wolves are sometimes more trouble than they're worth."

"Ha!" Earl barks. "They're no-good cow-killing varmints."

"This is their home, not ours," Walter counters. "They were here first."

Earl snorts his disapproval.

"Well, let's get moving," Walter says, obviously wanting to avoid an argument with Earl. "Earl, why don't you find a branch that Nat can use for a crutch?"

Earl walks off, grumbling. Walter looks at you and Nat and shrugs with a laugh.

Turn to page 25.

"As soon as Uncle Brad and Nat drive away, Aunt Lucy immediately notices the cut on your forehead. "Come here, sweetie. Let me look at that," she says. "Oh dear. Maybe you should have gone with Nat and your uncle to the doctor."

But the cut's not as bad as Walter thought, and Aunt Lucy takes you into the house to get it cleaned up.

Afterward, you and Muddy unload the chuck wagon, brush down the horses, and put away the rig. By the time you're finished, it's suppertime. Aunt Lucy serves a platter full of chicken-fried steaks, a huge bowl of mashed potatoes and cream gravy, and a big salad with home-grown greens and tomatoes. After the meal Muddy promises that tomorrow you'll get to bust some broncs. You're so excited you don't think you can sleep, but the moment you put your head to the pillow, you're out.

Turn to page 70.

102

You and Nat get to work setting up two large camp-fires. The beeves are still a couple of miles away, but the sound of their hooves rumbles through the valley. A quick chill runs down your spine, and you automatically pull your hands into your sleeves for warmth.

Nat sets up torches around the campsite. The air smells damp, so Nat pitches several tents for the crew to sleep in. Last night was dry, so everyone slept out in the open.

In the early dusk the range is strangely quiet. The birds have stopped singing, and the crickets and other night creatures haven't begun their calls.

You crouch by the fire and try to warm yourself. It isn't long before a rider breaks through the shadows into the light of the torches. It's Earl. He's covered in dust and looks exhausted.

"I must have swallowed half that prairie out there, riding behind those lead-footed beeves," he complains, whacking his hat against his leg to shake the dust off.

Turn to page 89.

You awaken in your own bed. Aunt Lucy sits in a chair beside you. She smiles when you open your eyes.

"How are you feeling, hon?" she asks.

You try to answer, but your throat is raw. The hot air in the barn has burned it.

Aunt Lucy smiles again and says, "You'll be fine. Doc says all you need is a little rest. I want to thank you for saving Uncle Brad's life. He said if you hadn't helped him out, he wouldn't have made it."

You manage a smile. You're glad Uncle Brad's not hurt.

Your aunt stands up and heads for the door. "I'm going to get you a big bowl of ice cream. That'll make your throat feel better."

You drop your head back on the pillow. This vacation is one that you won't forget for a long time.

The End

ABOUT THE AUTHOR

Laban Carrick Hill is the author of several titles in the Choose Your Own Nightmare series. He lives in Burlington, Vermont.

ABOUT THE ILLUSTRATOR

Eric Cherry's first artistic influence was his father, a Washington, D.C., police artist who taught him the basics of illustration while finishing his sketches at the dining room table. Eric lives in New York City, where he studies under Frank Mason at the Art Students League.